MR. MEN

ADVENTURE WITH

Pirates

Original concept by
Roger Hargreaves

Written and illustrated by
Adam Hargreaves

EGMONT

Mr Happy and his friends were sailing happily across the ocean on Mr Happy's yacht.

"This is the life," said Little Miss Sunshine.

Just then a shadow fell across the yacht.

At first Mr Happy thought it was a cloud, but when he looked round he realised that a ship had sailed up behind them.

A tall sailing ship.

A tall sailing ship with cannons sticking out of its portholes.

A tall sailing ship with the Jolly Roger flying from its mast.

"Farmers!" screamed Little Miss Scatterbrain in fear.

Well, they weren't farmers, they were pirates, but she was right to be scared.

It was the infamous Captain Yellowbeard.

The most ruthless buccaneering buccaneer of all buccaneers.

And when Mr Happy and his friends were hauled aboard the pirate ship they discovered just how ferocious Yellowbeard was.

"You have a choice," he snarled. "Join my crew or walk the plank!"

They all decided it was probably best to become a pirate.

Everyone except for Mr Impossible.

"I'll walk the plank," he said.

"Oh goody!" cried the crew.

But their pleasure was short lived.

When Mr Impossible reached
the end of the plank he did
not fall into the ocean.

He kept on walking.

In the air!

He did not even
wet his feet.

The rest of them soon realised what a hard life it was being a pirate. They had to get out of their hammocks before the sun was up in the morning.

Mr Lazy found it particularly difficult.

He kept getting into trouble for falling asleep.

He fell asleep scrubbing the deck.

He fell asleep climbing the rigging.

He fell asleep
at the ship's wheel.

He even fell asleep
out on the yardarm.

It was also all very confusing.

Everything aboard ship was called by a different name.

The kitchen was the galley, the back of the ship was the stern, and the front was the prow.

Poor Mr Dizzy was made the ship's cook.

He did not know whether he was coming or going.

Everyone wanted eggs for breakfast.

Oh dear!

Mr Dizzy was not the only one in a bit of a muddle.

Mr Wrong pointed his cannon in the wrong direction during firing practice.

They were aboard the pirate ship for a week before they learnt what Yellowbeard had in store for them.

It turned out that the pirates were searching for Blackbeard's treasure.

They had a map, which marked where Blackbeard's treasure-laden ship had sunk.

It also turned out that the pirates did not know how to swim.

So Yellowbeard wanted Mr Happy and his friends to dive down to the wreck and retrieve the treasure.

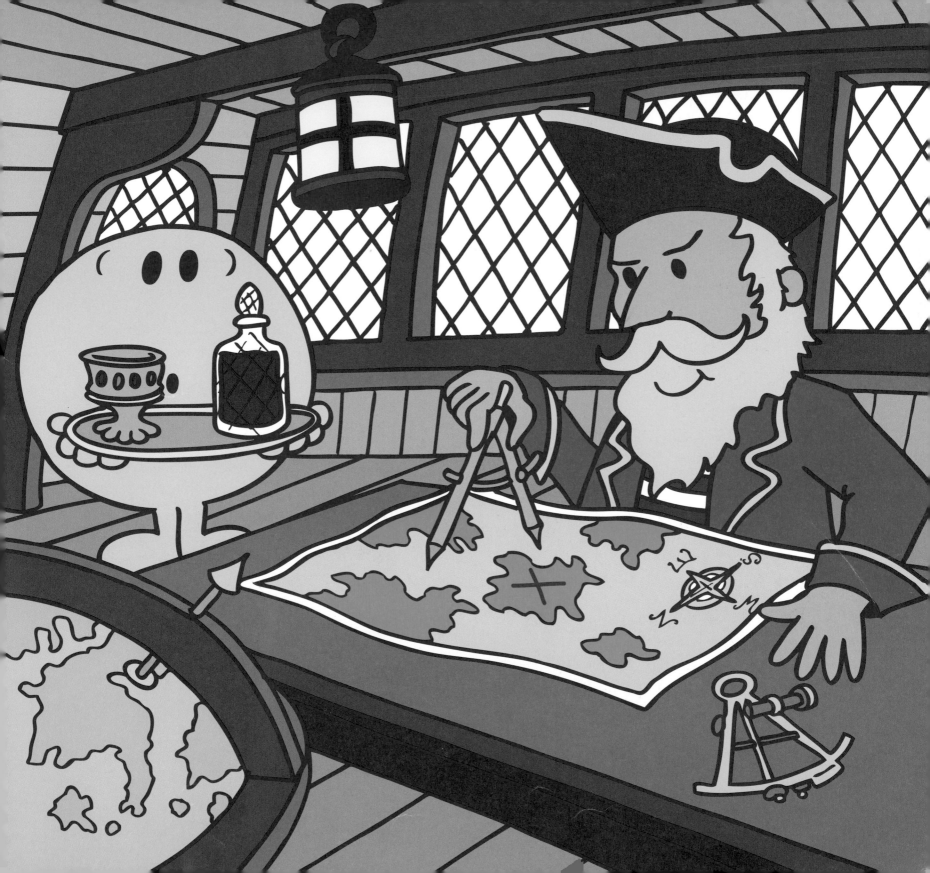

Blackbeard's ship had sunk off the coast of Skull Island and Mr Wrong was sent up to the crow's nest to keep a look out for the Island.

Eventually, after a lot of going round in circles, they found Skull Island.

Mr Happy and his friends had to put on diving suits and were then lowered to the wreck.

As the wreck came into view, Mr Happy saw that there were sharks circling it.

How were they ever going to get to the treasure?

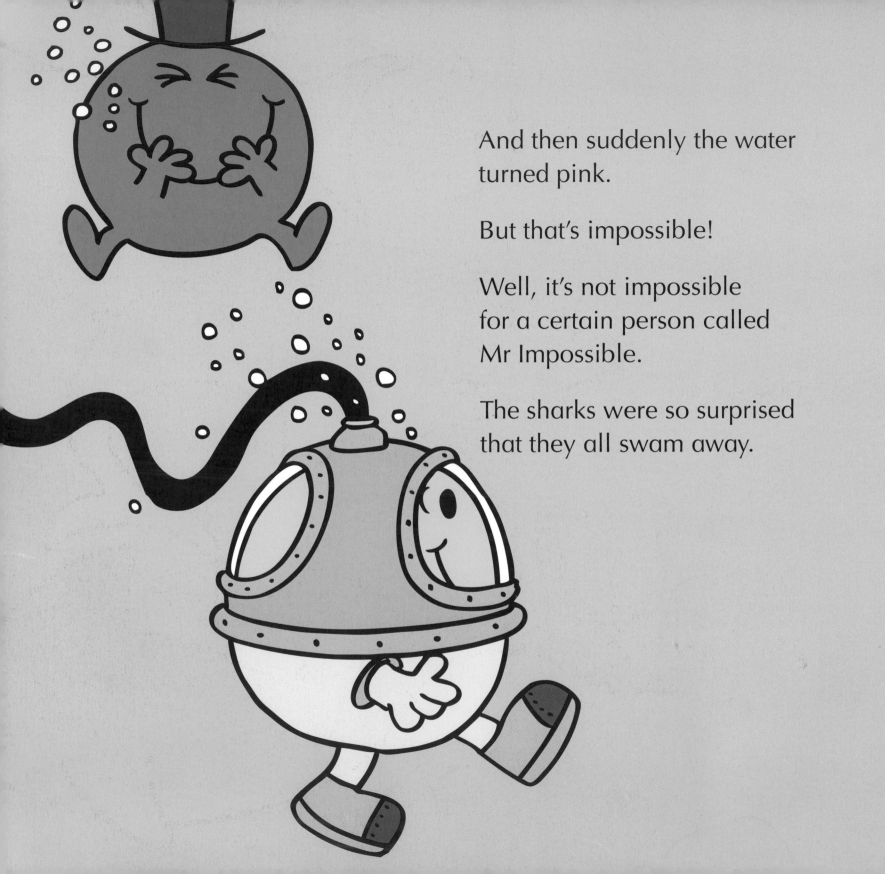

And then suddenly the water turned pink.

But that's impossible!

Well, it's not impossible for a certain person called Mr Impossible.

The sharks were so surprised that they all swam away.

The sharks had gone, but their problems were not over.

Mr Happy clambered through the rotting wreck until he found the treasure chest.

But it was not the chest that caught his attention.

What caught his attention was the giant octopus with enormous tentacles sitting on top of the chest!

However, the octopus' tentacles were no match for Mr Tickle's arms.

Within seconds Mr Tickle had the octopus tied up in knots and they were able to retrieve the treasure.

Once they had hauled the treasure ashore, Mr Forgetful was given the task of burying it to keep it safe.

He dug a deep hole, lowered the chest to the bottom and filled it in.

The pirates had gone off for an afternoon snooze while they waited for Mr Forgetful to finish the hard work.

"It's all done," said Mr Forgetful, waking the Captain.

"Excellent," said the Captain. "Where did you bury it?"
Mr Forgetful looked at Captain Yellowbeard and then
he looked at the long beach.

"I can't remember," he said.

The Captain was furious.

But not nearly as furious as when he realised that Mr Happy
and his friends had taken the long boat while they were
busy digging, and Captain Yellowbeard and the pirates were
marooned on Skull Island.

And Mr Happy and his friends continued their cruise aboard the pirates' ship.

"Hooray for Captain Happy!" they all cried.

"Hooray for Farmer Happy!" agreed Little Miss Scatterbrain.